Back Beat

by

Albert DeGenova and Charles Rossiter

Publisher/Editor: N. Blei

Layout Editor: Jan Mielke

Cover and inside pages art: Emmett Johns

Copyright: © 2001 Albert DeGenova and Charles Rossiter

ISBN: 1-889460-04-4

CROSS ✚ ROADS PRESS
P.O. Box 33
Ellison Bay, WI 54210

Intro Riff

Be It Beat

The Beat message became the only rebellion around — and it is still the same today...With the dot-commies and the whole computer consciousness, the Beat message is needed now more than ever.
— Ferlinghetti, Oct. 28, 2000

Be
beat
be it Beat.
Be as the beginning,
rhythm in time...
being, being there, beating.
beating time back.
Heart beating in the universe.
heya heya heya.a yo.ho yaha hahe.ya.an,
Native American Navaho chant
(Kerouacian OLD ANGEL MIDNIGHT tongue).
"All good things are wild and free," Thoreau's ear to the earth. "Give me
for my friends and neighbors wild men, not tame ones."
"The purpose of life seems to be
to acquaint man with himself," preaches Emerson.
"Life consists in what a man is thinking of all day."
Heart beat,
beat beat beat
beating the storylines of a country and its people,
individually, in unison, in time.
It's all the same generation,
the beat within.

"I celebrate myself and sing myself,

And what I assume you shall assume

For every atom belonging to me as good belongs to you.

I loaf and invite my soul," wails Whitman.

"Breathe the air but leave plenty after me."

After he, after we, after thee,

on the upbeat…Vachel Lindsay's drum:

"Mumbo-Jumbo will hoo-doo you.

Beware beware, walk with care,

Boomlay, boomlay, boomlay, boom.

Boomlay, boomlay, boomlay, boom.

Boomlay, boomlay, boomlay, boom.

Boomlay, boomlay, boomlay, BOOM."

Upbeat, downbeat, beatbeat, beatbeatBeat

"Drum on your drums, batter on your banjoes,

sob on the long cool winding saxophones.

Go to it, O jazzmen," Sandburg croons in the Chicago streets.

"I will be the word of the people…I will say everything."

(O jazzmen, O beatmen,

O bebop Bird, ah um Mingus, O blue Miles men,

beating in the waiting wings)

It's like it's all always coming together, man…

Enter: THE Beat, in their own time,

The word and world according to Then & Now.

The Beat all around as we breathe.

News Flash from the Cosmos: JACK'S BACK!

Subtext: HE NEVER LEFT THE ROOM.

Check today's poetry scene, performance & slam,

check the little mags & small presses,

the roads taken, the streets, the bookstores,

the angry pockets of America the Beautiful — bruised, broken, beat.

Jack's back and crackin', memorializing the moment.

"Where we going, man?"

"I don't know."

"…time to move on"….

Move on, man, but hear the Howl among us still:

Kerouac, Ginsberg, Waldsman, Corso, Kandel, Kaufman, Ferlinghetti,

Burroughs, Snyder, DiPrima, Cassady, Jones, Welch…

The heart of the Beat beats on…

The shadow of Patchen, past:

"I believe that to deliver myself

Is to deliver you."

The prayer of Kandel, historic-present:

"LET IT GO!

"IT NEVER STOPS MOVING"

Be your own breath beating Buddha—any Way you go.

Enter: the new millennium on a BACK BEAT,

two guys from then & now, DeGenova & Rossiter,

Beat and jazz inspired poets, hell-bent and holy heirs apparent of the

Word, spoke, writ, beat to a time that will not die.

Enter, too, afterthoughtfully, O'Leary, with her LITTLE BITS OF TRUTH

(a separate CR + Press Broadside) remembering the beat of the Beat

women who were there and not there — but here finally once and for all.

All together now:

The Beat in the beginning is now and ever shall be,

Ah, man!

— Norbert Blei
Europe Lake
December, 2000

Beat Ba-Lues

By

Albert DeGenova

Acknowledgements

Grateful appreciation and acknowledgement is made to the following magazines and anthologies where some of these poems first appeared: *The Café Review, Fresh Ground, U-Direct, VIA (Voices of Italian-Americans), After Hours, DotNet* (online anthology), *Sunlight on the Moon* (anthology), and *Poetry Motel*.

About the poet

Albert DeGenova grew up in Chicago and now lives in Oak Park, IL, on the same block that Ernest Hemingway spent his youth. He is a blues saxophonist and poet by night, a marketing communications professional by day...one of those poets lucky enough to be able to use his writing talents to earn a living. He was an editor of the *Oyez Review,* and has recently launched a new literary/arts journal *After Hours* where he wears the hats of publisher and editor. Al is also half of the performance poetry duo AvantRetro (wth Charlie Rossiter) that performs throughout the greater Chicago area.

Dedication

To Norb, for his support, enthusiasm, and wisdom

To Pat Hertel, for her unwavering friendship and poetic insights

To Eden, my Baubo...

SWEET BELLY

O Baubo,
Greek belly goddess
who laughed away Demeter's despair,
headless
you live without regret
your hips, your limbs, your belly
lead you —
look at me through nipple eyes
psychic eyes
that sense fear, anger, cold, noise
arousal —
speak to me
from the deep mine between your legs
that tells truth unadorned
unencumbered, sacred, sensual
that breathes full and long
and feels, feels, feels
sensations unknown —
tell your stories of the fertile earth
the muck of the psyche,
dirty jokes and belly laughs
that loose all control.

O Baubo
dirty, belly goddess
come laugh with me and be my love
and we shall
life's pleasures know.

"...A naked lunch is natural to us,
 we eat reality sandwiches.
 But allegories are so much lettuce.
 Dont hide the madness."

— Allen Ginsberg 'On Burroughs Work'

I didn't know that eating 79¢ burritos from Taco Fiesta on south Wabash in Chicago (because what I had in my pocket was $2) was beat. I didn't know that my young just-out-of-college head had been turned inside out, that my self-confidence, my dreams were gone...that being beat would turn who I had been, or thought I had been, a full 180 degrees to the outside, the ba-lues side, the dark side, the soul side, the go-gotta-go-go side of a high-speed shuffle rhythm at 3 a.m. on stage with Lefty Dizz at the Kingston Mines. I just didn't know that being beat would lead me to the northside blues of Chicago's nighthawks, and Wild Turkey, and easy women with sad pouting faces, and poems that would pour from my pen more than 10 years later.

I hadn't yet read Kerouac's definition of beat—

It's a kind of furtiveness...Like we were a generation of furtives. You know, with an inner knowledge there's no use flaunting on that level, the level of the "public," a kind of beatness—I mean, being right down to it, to our selves, because we all really know where we are—and a weariness with all the forms, all the conventions of the world."

...or Times Square street hustler Herbert Huncke's definition—

"exhausted, at the bottom of the world, looking up or out, sleepless, wide-eyed, perceptive, rejected by society, on your own, streetwise."

In 1981 I never considered the metaphysical, never considered karma, never thought that it was no coincidence that I should find my voice inside blues and jazz and a roach-infested bathroom...never considered what astrologers might have to say about the fact that Ginsberg's HOWL facing a federal court and Kerouac's ON THE ROAD and Sonny Rollins' WAY OUT WEST all happened in the same year that I was born, 1957. Never thought that maybe someday someway this place of beatness would lead me on my own road to a state of dharma bum-ness.

This is all hindsight of course. The sight of a poet who (at that time) couldn't write a poem to save his soul, though he tried, though he knew his soul needed some work, though he knew poetry could help those long nights of watching shadows move across cracked walls, who instead of a pen reached for his saxophone.

What I did know in 1981 was that I was on a journey, that I had entered a new

11

school, that my mind and life were empty and waiting to be filled. I knew that many of those empty spaces were being filled by a boss friend mentor, Herb Nolan, who would stand with a cup of coffee in hand telling tales, every morning, every afternoon, most of the day, in front of my desk in the offices of DOWN BEAT magazine—that icon of jazz journalism, that paid only slightly more than the poverty level, but allowed us to listen to records all day long and come in late if the music lasted too long the night before. I was completely aware that Herb's storytelling was leading me to one book after another, from one record to another. Herb had lived the Beat era and owned first editions of little known (in late 1970s college lit classes) and out of print classics. Herb was why I bought a copy of ON THE ROAD and why I studied SAXOPHONE COLOSSUS...my two points of entry into Beat writing and pure jazz improvisation.

Though I didn't recognize it as the turning point that would redirect my music and poetry, I had a crippling awareness of what had beaten me, what I couldn't wrestle to the mat, what gnawed at me like a demon ulcer. My spirit from my toes to my cock to my short-circuited brain was beat. I knew that the reason I had rented a furnished transient studio apartment where I peed in the sink to save a trip down the hall to a common bathroom, where the famed alleged

Tylenol killer lived in the next apartment, where I'd light the gas burners and oven of a small stove to shake the winter morning chill...the reason was because shortly after our second wedding anniversary I found someone else's wet semen in my first wife's panties. This, this was what I knew.

Missing You

Caffeine, nicotine, martini
cymbal sizzle
intoxication.
But I'm swingin'
I'm jammin'
I'm staring at the red-head dancin'
like she's the only one in the room...

and missing
you.

Bedroom dark
run my finger along
empty
wrinkled sheet
your hip
your thigh...

cock-hard
sighing.

Curbside urban campfire

rusting steel drum
yellow-orange dancing flames
seize me like compulsion.
Savage hot tongues lick, are
violent passion, are
consuming madness.
Broken 2x4s
fallen walls
submit
crack,
the wood
naked
vulnerable.
Ominous red ember heart
summons.

I miss you
mortally.

Findings On The Quest For Truth

Truth is an acquired taste
like straight bourbon or anal sex.

Truth hides in childbirth, betrayal, bigotry,
in an Ornette Coleman improvisation
in a Janis Joplin scream,
in the suicides of the great poets who
swallowed Truth whole
and found the taste like dandelion greens.

There is no Truth if not

chewed, scratched, sipped, sniffed, fucked,
eyeballed...

They say "the Truth will set you free"—
or it will fuck you up
'til you bleed poems,
'til wisdom strangles your soul,
'til the love in your heart
coughs up black blood
and dies.

The apartment I rented was on Belden
and Geneva, near Chicago's Lincoln Park, a
short walk to the lake. I moved in during
the winter when the dirty halls and walls
and old guys wearing grease-smeared pants
smelled of stale green loneliness. It
matched my mood. I hated it, resented it,
fought the nights alone by going for long
walks...walks that led to the Halsted Street
blues clubs. I read a notice about a Monday
Night Blues Jam at the Kingston Mines. It
took weeks to muster the courage to grab my
saxophone and check it out.
    At my first jam session I was paired up
with a young trumpet player, Jason, who sold
beer at Wrigley Field during baseball season.
He invited me to join him later that week
backing up Lefty Dizz. That was the start
of it. I played whenever I could, practiced
constantly, became a Mines regular. I'd walk
across the street to B.L.U.E.S and listen,
and sit-in, and breathe the smoky beer-soaked

air there until I had enough and then
moved back to the Mines. I jammed with who-
ever would have me, eventually I
actually made a little money on real gigs.
I learned when to play and when to not,
how to throw down a shot of bourbon to brace
up for a late set, how to make eye-contact
with the pretty ladies who loved the novelty
of a young white sax player, how to move
from winter to spring to summer on the growl
of a blues note, how to make home of an
end-of-the-line flophouse, how to appreciate
the beauty in hopelessness, the beauty in
living honestly.

Baby, Don't Ya Wanna Go

1.
X-Ray Blue borrows cymbals
tapes his drum kit together
MCs the Monday Night Blues Jam
bestows on me a blues name, "Bossanova."
Tattooed, dark glasses,
ladies' man
olive-skinned, thick-lipped
hustler
knows every musician, nightcrawler, dealer
knows the games
knows the tunes, knows the grooves.
Fast with his sticks, fast with a knife
and good with both.

2.
Lana drinks coffee when she's high
flicks ashes in the saucer,
lost her voice, can't keep time
lost her youth to the Blues
and drugs and booze and dreams
of Aretha Franklin stardom.

Lana licks her lips and
grinds her thighs at young white boys
like me.
"Love to watch you blow your horn."

Lana was a coffee 'n' cream-colored beauty
I can see it in the thin fragile hand
she holds out to me like a princess.

3.
Valerie is 21
black and beautiful
big voice, impassioned voice
big eyes, determined eyes
"I'm gonna be some-body.
Listen to me sing."

Believes only white men and women
can make her cum,
first disastrous road trip offers blow jobs
to prevent musician mutiny
then cries and tries to suppress the rumors.
And insists, "I'm gonna be some-body."
Uses my shoulder for comfort.

4.
I brush dry leaves from the couch and mattress
alley antiques of the furnished studio.
Here I live alone
on Belden Street
broke and single
again,
ragged dreams and
promises packed with yellowed paperbacks
in a milk crate that sits in a dusty corner.
Down the 15-watt bare bulb hallway
a common bathroom
shared by seven tenants,
water bugs on the walls,
dirty cracked linoleum,
neighbor smells,
neighbor hair in the tub,
no shower, no radiator, it's cold so cold.

5.
Neither heaven nor hell,
this Limbo absolutely doesn't matter.
So leave the turntable on all night
Archie Shepp plays sex soft sax
"Trouble In Mind" blues
she'll be gone in the morning
doesn't matter
white or black, thick or thin, there are no preferences
at 2 a.m. it doesn't matter
the same record works every time, perfectly timed
she'll be gone by morning
and I'll lay dry-sweat naked
alone at first light
her mascara on my pillow.

6.
Lucky lost his left ball to a bullet
shot on stage.

Lucky walks on the bar playing guitar
using a beer glass as a slide.

Lucky drinks Wild Turkey
'til his eyes go yellow
his voice goes hoarse
and his fingers miss the strings.

Lucky invites me to do a gig.
Hot humid summer Saturday in Chicago
playing hard, lips hurting swollen
sundown to sun-up it's standing room only.

Lucky leaves without paying me
his guitar player gives me a joint.
Dog-faced woman pays Lucky's tab
follows him home.

7.
Little Annie pierces her nipples, navel, labia;
adorns herself with tiny bells that
tinkle and tickle when she wiggles
that certain way
to control the wet
and waking dreams of
slobbering hound dog boys
so easily conditioned
who follow her home, prancing
tails high.

Then she is master
in control of her destiny.
Pain is submerged in pleasure's red sea
until the gray sunless morning when
despair floats to the surface
like bitter semen.

8.
At the far end of the bar
she sits alone smoking
anonymous
legs twisted into a French braid
arms knotted across her stomach
watching passing glances for prurient stares
that would penetrate her dark blue wool suit.
She puts out her cigarette
with a nervous, machine gunning wrist movement
staring into the powdered ashes
as if into a mirror,
sucks her ice cubes dry, and leaves.

9.
Transients all,
fifty tenants in furnished rooms
can hear my saxophone
some pound on the floors or radiator pipes.
Most don't care.

10.
Danny lives upstairs.
Unlocked door swings open as I knock.
He looks like any junkie sitting in his underwear
but the eyes,
the eyes, are dark, deepset black stones
watery, bloodshot
the eyes of death.
He washes down pills
with a quick-jerk swallow of old cold black coffee.
And the metamorphosis begins.
He pulls on dark blue pants
a pinstripe running the length of his leg,
buttons the light blue shirt, clips on a tie,
badge in place, lifts on a gun belt,
slides the dark glasses into place.

This is no ordinary cop. This is Codeine Cop,
chest buttons pulling like a god.

Danny moonlights.
Checks I.D.s, collects the cover charge.
Pockets what he can.

11.
When the Blues strikes, close your eyes and blow.
One-way roller coaster ride down, no stopping,
no getting off
a heart bursting rush like bad cocaine
addictive as morphine scratching every nerve end
the longer the fall, the longer the scream

and you're forced to cry out
uncontrolled as in orgasm
without thoughts, without sight
and your scream is music like none other.

Singer with the "Psycho" sweatshirt says,
"I'm about to sing somethin' y'all don't know a fuckin'
    thing about,"
and that's the whole point.

12.
Belden Street
your morning light warms me
as I put my horn down to unlock your door.
I cling to a passion found
in the dirt of no place to go.

I've ridden the roller coaster and must ride again.
"I'm your backdoor man,
I'm your hootchie cootchie man,
I'm a crosscut saw,
There's a red house over yonder,
Well come-on,
Baby, don't ya wanna go."

A letter from the building manager was slid under my door...drum roll in my head... rim shot echo through what was now home... I was evicted. I knew it was coming. No stopping the progress of real estate development, Chicago's gentry was moving in, what had been home to over 50 survivors of the streets and lost jobs and shit jobs and alcoholism was turned into six luxury condos. We all moved on.

I found a real apartment that cost real money. I joined a "jobbing" band that would contribute to my income, fell in love with the singer, got married, had two sons (Cole and Max), got a real job and built a career in marketing communications, I became a corporate working stiff. Yeah, I conformed to a middle class life. I was playing "New York, New York" and "Let Me Call You Sweetheart" at weddings and corporate parties in hotels, at country clubs...even my music became bourgeois.

Except that I could feel the blues rhythms and bass lines and guitar licks in my footsteps, that I could never play "Misty" without adding a little "something." Except that on my lunch hour I read Holmes' GO or Burroughs' JUNKIE or Ginsberg's KADDISH or Anne Sexton's letters, or Algren's MAN WITH THE GOLDEN ARM. I'd search out the City Lights bookstore or the Village Vanguard on business trips to San Francisco and Manhattan. My bohemian soul could not be evicted. How many white-collar corporate "ties" can take a group of salesmen out for a good time, bring 'em to a blues bar called Rosa's to see Grammy-winning Sugar Blue, talk to the star as an old friend, then go out to the car get a saxophone out of the trunk and sit-in with the band. That's what reputations are made of...that's how a round peg fits into a square hole.

(excerpt from Song For My Son)
#6

Writers' ghosts walk on Kerouac Street
Beat poems on beat up shelves
City Lights
stands unchanged (and not)
on the border between Little Italy and Chinatown.
Diane di Prima loses her virginity
again and again
as I sip espresso
with her MEMOIRS OF A BEATNIK.
I feel their sour breath;
the writers' ghosts of 1960 San Francisco
are wheezing, laughing, fucking, drinking
while I am here doing my duty
marketing communications
for the corporate god.

A saxophone calls me into Chinatown
(wheezing voice of the poets).
Oh spirits, we are kindred
in this dirty, old, beautiful, alive, dead
city with the bridge
yet I
am a conspicuous,
lamenting conventioneer tourist,
part-time poet, part-time saxophonist, who
chose the path
more traveled.

Cole, listen to the poets.
Listen..."to thine own self be true."
Listen..."Blow, man, blow!"

As I watched my first son come into this world to breathe and grow and learn and challenge me to be a better man, my poetry was reborn as well...so much truth in the hungry cry of a baby.

But I had changed, my writing had changed, there was a new rhythm to my words. My head was and is filled with echoes of X-Ray Blue's drums and Joe Kelley's wild loco-motive abandonment on guitar and Big Time Sarah's big-as-the-house voice. And in there too...so many writers...Algren, Hemingway, Sexton, Plath, Ginsberg, Snyder, Rexroth, DiPrima, Neruda and Kerouac, especially Kerouac, and all the others. But who's to say what influenced what. Did I read ON THE ROAD or GO to know how to act on Halsted Street at midnight on a Saturday night a saxophone and blonde cutie in tow? But the reading led to more reading, it spoke to me just as Miles Davis and Sonny Rollins and Muddy Waters and Albert Collins and John Coltrane and Junior Wells all spoke to me in their own languages. You live your life day to day, you empty and refill, you go numb and learn new sensations. You love and learn to love again and again.

You cannot write "one true sentence" unless you've lived it...second-hand reportage lacks the edge of the razor, the growl of the tenor saxophone. The Beats lived what they wrote, no bullshit...they had respect, a reverence for the stories and the poems they told, the characters they created. Ginsberg's "I saw the best minds of my generation destroyed by madness, starving hysterical naked..." speaks an elegy of sincerity, of love...his tale of his mother's institutionalization and death in KADDISH brought me to tears with their loving longing affection. In his words I felt the truths of my own life again...truths wearing new masks.

Demons dressed in clinical depression moved into our home and covered all the windows all the art of our life all our laughter with heavy purple muslin. You don't have to live in an alley to be hopeless, lost, beaten.

Suicide

Today I read my wife's suicide note.

Her letter spoke softly, gently caressing.
All the love she had held back
was saved for this one letter,
as if with this last kiss
she could erase the pain of living
the pain of leaving
and walk quietly away.

My words could not lift
the black shroud,
could not dull
the blade,
nor flush the pills.
And I cry
when truth lays death naked,
when I stand impotent
in the shadow of
"love is not enough."

Living With Witches

I cry when you're crazy
when you scream in my face
when you can't smile
when everywhere is a room without doors
that, by necessity, was built from the inside out
but there is no out.
Unless
"you look in the mirror, see what you saw,
take the saw and cut your way out."
The answer to a childhood riddle, simple,
all a matter of your point of view.
But you
always see the glass half empty.

I see the same glass nearly spilling over
and I cry when you're crazy.

    * * * * *

I believe the good witch of Idyllwild
who sold me faerie dust to lighten the heart
happiness to sprinkle on your pillow.
Sweet dreams.
And if the happy dreams don't come
I hold you through your nightmares.

    * * * * *

There is the selfish witch of Morton Grove
who stole your childhood
greedy thief in mother's clothing.

The woman who bore you and forgot the pain
who cannot tell you whether you had measles

or chicken pox
and doesn't care.

The woman who had no use for a second daughter.
Useless you, never good enough, insignificant.

The woman who taught you to cry without sobbing
without a sound, without movement
tear tracks line your cheeks like scars
you hide your sadness with uncanny skill.

This is the witch jealous of your successes
who taught you that your glass is always half empty.

    * * * * *

Then there is the unseeing witch of the world
who sews a costume you must wear
but doesn't fit you well.
You squeeze your breasts
your hips, stretch your arms
and legs, cover your face.
This woman's suit twists you
forces you to limp and hurts
hurts deep into your muscles
deep into the part of you that will always fight
but you cannot shed the clothes of your role.
You pull and tear, contortionist in a straightjacket
struggling to escape
to strip naked
to be woman that you are for all to see your beauty and
imperfection
struggling not to succumb
not to be shrivelled, numb, faceless.

    * * * * *

There is also the relentless, brutal witch of guilt
sadistic sitting on your shoulder
who cuts notches in your ribs
for each mistake, every weakness
pummelling your self-esteem
forcing you to bruise yourself
masochistic
whipping your own heart
blaming yourself
for the sharp cruelty of the predators
preying on your vulnerability.

The witch who teaches the words,
"I am unworthy,"
"I cannot know happy."

And I cry
knowing you are good,
sweet lamb.

     * * * * *

And then there is the unforgiving witch within
dressed in depression
who drains your life like a vampire
like a virus
until you are empty.
She is the powerful witch
strength like God
who leads you to Hell
or worse, Limbo
where nothing is all there is
who steals your eyes and ears
so that visions of
summer sun-showers and
sunsets on California beaches

and the sound of your son's laughter
are silent blackness

And I cry for you
when you're crazy.

     * * * * *

But oh, there is a love witch
in me in you in our son
in our unborn child.
This witch, barred from your youth,
you watch from the corner
of your eye through
a smoky cloud of mistrust.

This gentle witch who with subtle gestures
can guide your hands, your eyes,
your heart
who can teach you to
live with witches.

The witch who makes me sing encouragement
undying faith in your strength
like a cheerleader at the close of a losing game

the game you must win.

The witch who keeps me crying
arms around you when you're crazy.

She did heal....I healed. We turned another page, started sleeping in sunlight again. Two round pegs that laugh at not fitting into any square ol' hole, that still wonder at the paradox of the human spirit so like a Phoenix rising from the ashes of despair.

Camping with my sons, hiking in the Sierra Nevadas, conversing with the sun and the tall cedars of northern Wisconsin, I've come to feel a sense of identity with Dharma Bums and the Beat movement into Buddhism. It is amazing to realize how truly religious, how spiritual the Beats really were. John Clellon Holmes wrote, "What differentiated the characters in ON THE ROAD from the slum-bred petty criminals and icon-smashing bohemians that became something of a staple in much modern American fiction—what made them beat—was...Kerouac's insistence that actually they were on a quest, and that the specific object of their quest was spiritual." What struck Holmes—and later generations of readers like me—as the most moving, most inspirational quality of ON THE ROAD was the energy of its affirmative tone.

Kerouac redefined "beat" as the root of beatific "trying to be in a state of beatitude, like St. Francis, trying to love all life, being utterly sincere and kind and cultivating 'joy of heart.'"

"...Yet it was as a Catholic, it was not at the insistence of any of these 'niks' and certainly not with their approval either, that I went one afternoon to the church of my childhood...and suddenly with tears in my eyes and had a vision of what I must have really meant with 'Beat' anyhow when I heard the holy silence in the church (I was the only one in there, it was five p.m., dogs were barking outside, children yelling, the fall leaves, the candles were flickering alone just for me), the vision of the word Beat as being to mean beatific...There's the priest preaching on Sunday morning, all of a sudden through a side door of the church comes a group of Beat Generation characters in strapped raincoats like the I.R.A. coming in silently to 'dig' the religion...I knew it then."

—Jack Kerouac, excerpt from "On the Origins of a Generation" published in PLAYBOY, June 1959.

I discovered BIG SKY MIND: BUDDHISM AND THE BEAT GENERATION (Riverhead Books, Carole Tonkinson, ed.) And finally understood where a lot of Beat writing was coming from especially the concept of "spontaneous prose."

"...your singing or your chanting or your poetics is as neutral, impersonal, and objective as the wind through the black oak leaves, then you wouldn't have to be ashamed of expressing yourself because it's not yourself, it's

33

just the wind, it's just wind, it's just breath going through you.

"...I was writing a spontaneous chain poem with Chogyam and he said, and we finally agreed, 'First thought is best thought.'....that is to say, the first thought you had on your mind, the first thought you thought before you thought, yes, you'd have a better thought, before you thought you should have a more formal thought-first thought, best thought."
                    -Allen Ginsberg, excerpt from a lecture given in his "Spiritual Poetics" class at the Jack Kerouac School of Disembodied Poetics, Naropa Institute, July 29, 1974.

It makes me laugh, now, to write this narrative and see the parallels of my reading and writing and life. I've never consciously tried to write like anybody. I've never considered myself a "beatnik." Everything we live, do, say, read, hear, feel becomes a part of our soul.
  For me, nothing pulled all these concepts, these influences, these "-isms" of Zen, Beat, Jazz into one statement of the creative process as well as this quote taken from an essay titled "Improvisation In Jazz" written by Bill Evans and used for the liner notes for Miles Davis' KIND OF BLUE released in 1959...

"There is a Japanese visual art in which the artist is forced to be spontaneous. He must paint on a thin stretched parchment with a special brush and black water paint in such a way that an unnatural or interrupted stroke will destroy the line or break through the parchment. Erasures or changes are impossible. These artists must practice a particular discipline, that of allowing the idea to express itself in communication with their hands in such a direct way that deliberation cannot interfere. The resulting pictures lack the complex composition and textures of ordinary painting, but it is said that those who see will find something captured that escapes explanation. This conviction that direct deed is the most meaningful reflection, I believe, has prompted the evolution of the extremely severe and unique disciplines of the jazz or improvising musician..."

Close your eyes and blow. One note after another, one word after another...this is direct deed, this is the art in your veins. Just close your eyes and blow. I write because I have to, I play saxophone because I have to, I love because I have to, I cry because I have to...and so, the poems come whispering in my ear, sliding through the keys of my horn, tripping me in the dark, splashing like waves against my skinny-dipping ass.

Angels Got the Blues

Oh Lord show me the answer
Oh Lord oh show me the answer
Oh Lord send Gabriel to lead me
let angels take my hand

●

This guardian angel
(the faceless one) offers me
a cigar
which he pulls delicately
from a black leather case.
I smoke as
he plays piano
harsh chords filled with
black keys sounding
like a Monk-blue January day
like Manhattan at dawn.

"This is the sound of your soul"
he says. "Listen to it"
he says. "Know it"
he says.

I trust him
he has shaken me many times
as I've driven sleep-blind head-on
toward steel guard rails, or
toward truck mud flaps embossed
with naked women.
The heavy smoke
dances in his strange music
a weary limping waltz.

I listen, restless
shifting positions,
he plays
black keys
Monk-blue.

•

Deep greens and blues are the colors I choose
won't ya let me go down in my dreams
and rock-a-bye sweet baby James

•

Max does a cartwheel dance
across the dewy grass
through a fog
that wraps us in springtime.
"the clouds"
Max says "have come down to play
to pinch our cheeks to tickle our ears"
He is a four-year-old guardian angel
new at the job and always giggling.
"Look, above the broccoli trees,
there's an accordion moon playing 'bye, bye, my baby
bye, bye' and I
am going to eat
colors
sunrise cereal
don't even try to stop me!"
He pulls me through his playground
where jungle gyms are fantastic submarines
where red tulips stretch and scratch their bellies
and rocking horses play under umbrellas
where flying is as simple as letting go the swing.

•

Rock me baby, rock me all night long,
Rock me baby, rock me like my back ain't go no bone

•

My guardian angel says
    "to know me,
    fuck me, slow"
as she crawls over me
her pussy like a wet tongue
licking my stomach.
Her mouth against my cheek
chilling me with
muted trumpet voice,
    "fuck me, slow
    bite my apple, taste
    my salt. Don't
    rush my song.
    Inhale me like a Dominican cigar
    like Mexican weed
    taste each breath, smell
    the earth in me.
    I am the mountains of Utah
    the surf of Cozumel
    the steam rising from Chicago subways.
    I am crystal white winter morning."
My guardian angel says,
    "Fuck me
      slow."

•

stand
like a hummingbird
  the journey
inward
   is as long as the journey
     outward

He is the monk who
stands in my shadow
wearing an army surplus
overcoat
wrapped tight
his hands deep in the pockets.
He is Ben Zen, he is
Linus
the philosopher guardian angel
a priest with undying
faith
in me, a faith
that says the setting sun
means another tomorrow.
I wait for the
sunrise
in darkness.
He sweeps the words
like mouse droppings
out of the corners
of my mind, my ears
my pockets
and shows me the
poetry that is.
He is the dharma angel
who leads my hands
to the stones

bleached by sunlight, smoothed
by the untiring waves...
stones
become a waterfall
in my garden
where sparrows sing
at sunset.

Picture of Eden

You lay naked
on this million-year-old rock,
thigh of mountain
that bares its boulder knee
for you to rest against
in the sun
under towering summits,
a stream skipping over fallen trees
within reach of your thirsty toes.
You who heard the wolf-call echo
in your dreams, the screams
in your nightmares,
lay naked
here
on this stone chaise lounge
your full breasts bared to suckle
your babies, a garden, your truths—

and complete this picture
of you
in my mind

the sun on your belly
your eyes shut
to the black witches within who
had bound your touch in
coarse darkness.
You
who fought for sunshine
who dug in the earth to
deserve the peace in herbal tea and blue dawn—

should be
laying here
naked
the sun on your belly.

Kiss Me Again

Kiss me a
December snowflake
cool and wet
that warms on my cheek
that appears a lingering tear.

Kiss me a
midnight moonbeam
white and soft
that all-night dances through our room
to music that leaves me dreamless
breathless.

Kiss me again
an amber afternoon

of autumn silence
   comfortable as this old wool sweater
   as so many days yet before us,
of falling red leaves
   sad like so many days behind us
and smiling too
like so many days
   behind us.

Woman With Barbie Doll Hair

Woman with Barbie doll hair
plays bongos
rhythms without tempo
locks the small drums between
her legs like a Latin lover.
Her blind eye looks away, the other
glares a piercing stare.
"illusion delusion, allusion to a dream"
she chants
at brightly colored vacationers who
rush past her
to the end of the Key West pier
they raise plastic cups
Rum Punch and Margaritas
to celebrate the daily Sunset Festival.
"illusion delusion, allusion to a dream"
she continues
raising her empty tip jar
toasting her distant audience.
"Cuba is only 90 miles away,
you can swim it,"
she urges.

Listening

she straddles a wooden chair
backwards,
can smell the breath of the saxophone
closes her eyes
imagines sitting in a city fountain
wet skirt wrapped
against
around
thighs open
to the coolness
to the wind
head
thrown back
hair
long black in
thick strands like fingers
that touch "oooh right there"
lips eyes cheeks
smiling at
no
one
no
thing.

The Soul of the City

To look down upon the Old Town Square of Prague
from the Clocktower built centuries before "jez" music
made its way out of Storyville whore houses
and feel the sultry steamy sentiments that

surround New Orleans in my mind
because a band of street musicians play
Dixieland jazz with a Bohemian accent
in the center of the square and
overpower the Baroque melodies of a lonely boy
with his recorder who plays on a corner
near a café where Mozart finds his way
through speakers defiantly filling the spaces between
breaths of the Satchmo-esque trumpet,
this, this is the irony that gets
the old square's statues
of saints, and kings, and musicians, and artists,
and heroes
closing their eyes, covering their ears.

Yet as the tourists gather
at the foot of the Clocktower
everything stops on the hour, each hour,
when the clock performs its magical
mechanical dance
its centuries-old dance
bells chiming the beautiful irony of time.
As in Kafka's words, the gypsies' violins,
in the Gothic torture museum at the foot of a
sleeping castle,
as the man who dies in a nursing home
leaving no legacy,
as the adult child who remembers a father
as a bottle of vodka,
as with love betrayed,

the soul survives.

To Jimmy Santiago Baca,
In The House Tonight

The open-mic graffiti poets posture
for the Buddha, master in the audience.
He listens, applauds, drinks
bourbon.
But tonight
words swirl around the writer's head
like ice cubes in his glass, like
updrafts of circling snow outside.
He asks me to play,
play my saxophone
a song for his brother
the brother who died
just winter days ago.

"Play a song for me, play
a song for my brother
who was murdered.
Play a song because
there are things in a life
that you can't get over.
My mother was murdered
my father was murdered
and now
my brother —
there are things in a life
that you cannot get over."

He closes his eyes to say this,
he kisses his hands held as in prayer.
"Faith in the Virgin of Guadeloupe,

better than the trigger I pulled
the cold blood I shed
angry lives ago."

My fingers find the keys, stumble
into Amazing Grace
and spiral into a freefall of blue notes
that is a dead brother.
There are things in a life
you cannot get over,
things
that make
this poet's poems.
No burning need
for an open microphone
or polite applause
only the request
for a song
this January night—
there are things in a life
you cannot get over.

On Telling The Truth

Better
to be like
Paul Desmond who
never took off his tie
than to lie in the dark
high
wearing nothing but a rubber band around your wrist
that reminds you that you have

forgotten
something,
that you have surrendered
to the loneliness of K-Y
in the dark
alone,
that the sharp edge of Truth
has cut too close to the bone
despite you ripping open your shirt
despite those poetic purges
that swirl in the midnights of
nightmares black as Chopin.

Better
to be like Paul Desmond who
never took off his tie or let
his saxophone cry, the smooth tone
so controlled, phrases that didn't lie.
Or did they.
Were the screams tucked in with his starched
white shirt, the collar
only loose enough to let him blow
cool...
Desmond's demons buttoned up
in stiff white cotton.
Cool
too cool —
famous
and well-liked
unthreatening
in a safe white Oxford.
No one names his delirium
or cares if he told lies
or truths.

Better to lie alone in the dark
wearing nothing but a rubber band.

Last Supper

The day I met Jesus
he wore a black frock coat
woven from the coarse fiber of Chicago alleys.
He sat alone
a corner table
the McDonald's dinner crowd keeping its distance.
He spread a paper napkin
smoothing the edges
meticulously, ceremoniously
with fingers only partially clean.
He unwrapped a hamburger
placing it gently on the napkin
as if onto white linen.
He lifted steaming coffee
with two hands
passed it under his nose
eyes closed.
First bite brought a cough
a retch, pain
Jesus was a sick man.
He looked into my eyes
intimately.
He ate slowly, carefully
all he had
sat in front of him
I stood to leave
placed three dollars on his table

all I had.
He bowed his head as
I walked past him
out into December sleet
wrapping his stare inside my coat
a peculiar blessing.

Satori

Easy to be an atheist in Las Vegas
in a cosmos of jelly bean light
manufactured to delight greed
    easy to be an atheist
in suburban subdivisions where
cornstalks and farmhouses
lay entombed in concrete
    easy to be an atheist
where soil is only dirt
the soul starved
of poetry and tomatoes;

easy to not be, easy to
not be
not easy to be;

yet
a horse runs in New Mexico
a laughing woman on his back
his black mane, her long brown hair flying
freeing the wild madness within;

yet

stars fall
one after another, a
warm rain of summer dreams
finding two friends making wishes
on a rooftop in Prague;

yet
a man stands alone in a pine forest
facing the sun, blinded,
speaks to trees who know
this is where God lives
he cries to the light
praying for his children

spring water washes away cynicism
this baptism
at the altar of birch majesty
consummates a marriage to the Earth
and her waters

he lays naked, warmed on a river rock
his head on a daypack aromatic with
provolone, sausage and need
his senses feast on Neruda
words that exhaust him, he sleeps
the lake sings the ancient songs

to be to be to be
full of grace
the light
within thee.

Back There

go
gotta go-go
go
gotta go-go
4 speeds forward and no reverse
pass a 21st century hobo
dharma bum with rooster hair
backpack full of stories
to tell
tell of the road
the road back there
there
the hitchhiker I missed
back there, the stories
I missed
some
    where

Love Me Now

By

Charles Rossiter

Acknowledgements

Some of the poems in *Love Me Now* first appeared in *Paterson Literary Review; Underwood Review; Fractals...In the Arts; LIPS; Milwaukee Bugle-American; Backroads Gathering; Modern Haiku; Chronicles of Disorder; Baby Connection News Journal, Open Mic: The Albany Anthology; Life in Washington, D.C.*

About the poet

Charlie Rossiter is host and co-producer of the international audio poetry website, **poetrypoetry.com.** His other recent publications are *What Men Talk About*, which won the First Annual Red Wheel Barrow Prize from Pudding Press and *On Reading the 1,000 Year Sorrows in a Book of Chinese Poems* (Esker Press). His work has appeared in anthologies such as *Identity Lessons*, (Penguin) and *Passionate Hearts*, (New World Press). He performs nationally as a solo artist and as 1/3 of 3 Guys from Albany and around the Midwest as 1/2 of the performance poetry duo, AvantRetro. He has received an NEA Fellowship for poetry and is a Pushcart Prize Nominee. His touring has been supported by the New York Foundation for the Arts and the Ohio Arts Council.

Dedication

This one's for all the folks who've helped me develop the craft: Jeff Winke who provided an important early push back in Milwaukee; Robert Farr whose craziness helped me stay sane in D.C.; the highly critical and helpful Every Other Thursday Night Poetry Workshop in Albany (Jill Hanifan, Tess Lecuyer, Bob Elmendorf, Lori Anderson and all the rest); Allen Ginsberg and Gary Snyder for the workshops; and my performance buddies who are a constant spur to creativity (Dan Wilcox and Tom Nattell, the other 2/3 of "3 Guys from Albany," and Al DeGenova the other half of AvantRetro). And, as always, for Mary Ellen who makes it all possible.

The truth is such a rare thing it is delightful to tell it.
    — Emily Dickinson

In The Beginning. . .

So I moved to the Chicago area in late 1996 from Albany, NY and I'm missing my performance poetry group, 3 GUYS FROM ALBANY, cause we used to do a couple gigs a month and we had a lot of fun travelling around doing our poetry and meeting lots of interesting people. I hate travelling out-of-town for solo gigs. You do your thing, the folks are nice, but hey, they all know each other and you're an outsider so it's usually a little polite, goes-nowhere conversation and then the folks drift away to gossip about local people and issues. Afterward there's the late drive home or a solo motel overnight. I continued to perform as part of 3 GUYS FROM ALBANY, still do, but it's tough being 800 miles apart. We only get out on the road a couple times a year. I needed something local.

Then, along comes Al DeGenova and I can't believe my good luck. He's a wild saxophonist and get-down poet interested in performance poetry. So we team up and give ourselves the name, AvantRetro to suggest that we're artsy, contemporary guys with an affinity for our poetic forebears. "One eye on the future, one foot in the past," as we say when we perform. The idea of having a group name and getting up a show is to increase the fun of performing and make it easier to squeeze bucks out of places like Borders that think nothing of paying musicians, but think poetry is a *pro bono* art form.

When Al and I do our thing, people say the "Retro" part is obvious; they hear an echo of the Beats in what we do. So here I am, looking at my life and poetry, and connections to the Beats and their friends and the Beat poetic, trying to figure out what I might say about that, what I don't need to say, and how I can say something worthwhile without distracting from the poems. I'll just start at the beginning, but don't worry, we'll leap through time once we get rolling.

My background is Catholic, blue-collar Baltimore. Our neighborhood, Morrell Park, sat on a hill overlooking downtown, separated from it by a large public park and a "car barn" where the transit company stored buses and trolley cars in the old days. We were technically in the city, but the neighborhood was more like a village. My grandmother lived there in the same house for over 50 years and was a big part of my childhood. Today people tell me they detect a nostalgia in my poetry, a longing for the good old days. That's something you also find with the Beats, at least Kerouac and Ferlinghetti. To read Jack, you'd think tv hadn't been invented when he was writing. It's old-time radio that fascinates him. And Ferlinghetti is more likely to refer to Charlie Chaplin in a poem than somebody contemporary. Gary Snyder, of course, specializes in the long perspective.

Forget TV

In past was no tv
in the future none also
galvanic skin communication
connects all beings
in a net of wonder,
channel numbers become antiques
millions contract blue velvet syndrome
write words on bare bellies
pretty and smooth
501s unbuttoned to the crotch hair

Our Way

Outside the American dream
we haunt highways and streetcorners
through dirty blues and doo wop days
barrooms and coffeehouse nights
we search for friends, for truth, for love
on feather beds and oriental rugs
in dim cafes
barefoot on burning sand
we raise a glass
to electric skies gone crimson
we honor the days, the times
the ways of ancestors long gone
   who made us who we are
     who we are

My Nan

My Nan she got up at five
My Nan she ran clothes through the ringer
My Nan she ironed all the shirts
My Nan she stretched curtains on the stretcher

IF IT WAS A SNAKE IT WOULDA BIT YOU

My Nan she made the best dumplings
My Nan she rolled cookies on the metal top table
My Nan she dried noodles on the bed
My Nan she fixed ox tail soup
My Nan was an immigrant's daughter

FOLKS IN HELL WANT ICE WATER

My Nan had nine brothers and sisters
My Nan she had only one husband
My Nan was 50 years in one house

I PITY THE WOMAN WHO MARRIES YOU

My Nan she turned off the lights
My Nan she clipped coupons from the paper
My Nan she walked or rode buses
My Nan she gave soup to the neighbors
My Nan she went to third grade
My Nan she taught me to cook

WANT TO HAVE FUN—PICK UP A HORSE TURD
AND RUN!

My Nan she taught me canasta
My Nan knit me sweaters and mittons

My Nan she put on the band-aids

YOU'LL BE SORRY WHEN I'M DEAD AND GONE

My Nan her name was Theresa
My Nan she lived to eighty-seven
My Nan she died in our house

Listen

I'm the voice of the old ways
that can take you back to the days
of grandparents when things were
one telephone and one tv set
per household, wringer washers
78 rpm, ice boxes and victrolas
and the folks who owned cars
were on top of the world.

I'm the voice of the unpaved road
dusty, pock-marked and ribbed
by spring rain. I can take you places
the long straight interstate
never imagined where the air is clear
and the woods are deep,
places that make you want to
throw your head back
look up at the stars
and breathe.

I'm the voice of the front porch
where you can sit sipping iced tea

and talk to the neighbors
and your children about nothing
but the day behind you
and the night ahead
as the world slips by.

I'm the voice of your own music
that doesn't need an agent
or a stage or even a microphone.
I'm the song inside you that talks about
where you've been and how you feel.
I'm the high note you can't quite reach
but sing out anyway, long and loud.

I'm the voice of the hearty handshake
the arm around the shoulder
and the straight-forward look in the eye
that says hello friend, we're here together
you and me, let's enjoy it
while we can.

Beware

We who have kept our eyes open
are the last indiginous people of the 20st Century.
Regardless of Afro-Euro-Latino-Asian-Indio
grandmothers, we are together in this
because we are together endangered. Beware

. . . of smiling corporations bearing gifts.
Make no mistake, Starbucks is our Cortez

Bordello's Books & Music is our Custer
Big Brother's got 99 channels and rising
Wal-Mart comes bearing diseases many
are not immune against. Their parking lots
and paychecks are contaminated and spread
the infection. If you don't believe it,
look around. Small town America is sick
and dying, withered from a lethal dose. Beware.

People once thought you could not sell
the land because it belongs to everyone
and the Great Spirit, but the land got sold
to those who knew they could buy it with
tricks and mind-numbing gifts and then
they fenced it so it belonged to no one.
They do the same thing with your mind. Beware.

There are those who believe they are free
but their overstuffed asses are chained
by PizzaHut, Citibank, Microsoft
DunkinDonut chains to tv armchairs,
decapitation-hacksaw-gangrape movie houses
machine gun computer games, sick packs
of lite beer and snack bowls of empty
chemicals with names they can't pronounce. Beware.

Spitting poems in dark cafes is not enough.
We must act. Pull the plug and vote
with our folded wallets and watch their
bottom lines shrivel in a language they understand—
a ju-jitsu of the dollar as simple as turning off
the tv set
and astounding the Neilsen man when he
picks up the rating box and sees that it reads
"zero."

It's simple as grown-ups talking to kids
simple as a good book and homemade bread
simple as midnight skinny dips full of wet kisses
simple as not consorting with the enemy
simple as a trail hike
All over the world, we are everywhere
black, white, red, and brown
all over the world, they are everywhere
black, white, red, and brown.

    Beware

It's not the color or the cut of the clothes,
it's the consciousness

It's us against them
and we
      are our only chance.

Ah Youth...

College, now that was good times, or maybe
the best of times/worst of times. Parties, my
first big love, great sex, bopping around town
to art museums and coffee houses. Saw my
first play in college, heard my first
symphony, went to my first poetry reading,
heard poetry with jazz for the first time. It
was at the Magpie, a grubby little downtown
coffeehouse in D.C. Two hip-looking black guys,
one at the piano pounding bop, the other at
the mic putting out this fantastic poem
about a dog trotting freely in the street.

For years I thought that anonymous dude was one fine poet till I read the poem in CONEY ISLAND OF THE MIND. I was starting to read the beats about this time. In fact, I kicked off each summer with a re-read of ON THE ROAD. Usually on the beach at Ocean City.

This was the early 60s of civil rights marches, sit-ins. Stokley Carmichael led demonstrations on Maryland's eastern shore. We'd get stopped and searched by state troopers on our way down route 50 to the beach. All we had on us was beer and books. Usually we went in my buddy Mike's souped-up Ford Falcon with no back seat, just a collection of pillows. We lived on tomato sandwiches and Pabst Blue Ribbon. A pair of shorts, a couple sweatshirts, and a beach blanket was the wardrobe. Evenings we walked the boards in blankets like a couple of non-celebate monks looking for friendly women willing to take a chance. If we were lucky we slipped through the window of a rooming house. If not, we rolled up on the beach. (Kids, don't try this at home—wearing a blanket on the boardwalk in OC was outlawed long ago. Sleeping on the beach was always illegal.)

Around College Park, parties, cultural events and falling in love kept me busy. Dorm life was a psychological shock. It was the first time I'd been surrounded by people who'd been nowhere and whose sole goal in learning was to get a good job. The guys from the eastern shore were solid bigots and would have been happy to take a baseball bat to anybody sitting-in at their favorite back home diner. Interest in the arts was non-existent.

Junior year my buddies and I moved off-campus. That move probably saved my life. The alienation caused by the boredom of classes and the general dorm environment had me down as often as I was up from the great sex and art I was swimming in. We called our apartment the Bowery because it was basically a large dank basement room. The rent was cheap and we could walk across the tracks to a little store that had a perpetual sale on Pabst Blue Ribbon. Oh yeah, I majored in journalism because it offered the most electives. After College Park, I did grad school in Ohio. It was more of the same, but with more time in the library to keep up with the seminars.

Ocean City Summer

rooming house
windows over
the boardwalk
mom and pop
newspaper tourists

the blonde with the
dunes fire

I called her
moonlight
on the water
a labyrinth
of disciplines
and one we lived

A Sand Sculpted Crucified Christ

slips through his hands into
the white, red and green lights

at sunset, the tourist crowd
dependable as night begins

to gather, by the boardwalk's
edge, the red donation bucket

fattens, fathers in flat plaids,
mothers in popcorn sundresses

fascinated by the slow accumulation
of improbable sand grains into the

crucified christ they saw become before
their eyes the night before become again,

an almost audible sigh of expiration,
the crown of thorns, the curved and open

hands, it's a miracle on 3rd St.
you can almost hear the words

let them with eyes
to see, ears to hear : father why
have you forsaken me

sunday stained glass, hardwood
pews, incense aroma of salt and

seaweed, barefoot in yesterday's
clothes under an old army blanket

the artist beside his work seems
not to notice, the slow drift of

cruise ship lights offshore, the crowd,
the way occasional sand grains fall from

the face and hands and how we who are
without a god almost begin to believe

father forgive them,
forgive us, we know not and yet
begin to see

That Summer

I wanted to
tear your skin off
and wear you

I understood cannibals
when I saw you naked

and what parties we had

thighs and breasts
rose beyond mere clothing
upscale decadence
to us back then
meant having enough money
for airfare
to a legal abortion

Delbert in the tub
with the ice and beer
grinning through blue lips
he held court
with those of us who
deigned to pass
hellacious concoctions
in colors we'd only seen
in dreams

    let us fuck
our mutual brains out
to a little Vivaldi
    we'd say
let me feed your breath
    upon my thighs
my dear
in those days
we were friends who could be
counted upon
to water each other's flowers

we were easy on the geraniums
but the beds were another matter

Campus Politics

A woman in a plain black dress
was sucking a dashboard virgin mary
when we arrived, the plastic head
slipped between her lips,
came out and then went in again
to the tune of *In a Gadda Da Vida*
as she danced and hiked her dress,
made little fucking sounds and
pumped her hips. The men were
beardless, in gray slacks
and navy blazers.
The women were out of
Lord and Taylor and the drinks
and food and dope were free
compliments of Nixon and the GOP
who'd stocked their rented mountain cabin
with undercover young republicans
to make it with the college crowd.

I'd like to say we all got off
that night but no such luck.
Those Lord and Taylor women
were all tease and
not about to fuck for us
so we drank ourselves into
a state of grace and on the way out
by the side door
ripped off another case
went back to campus and laid down
on the lawn, woke up
at the crack of dawn hungover
we staggered home to sleep it off
and one week later cast our puny votes

for Humphrey and cursed the fates
when Nixon won.

graduate school

janis joplin raged
on jukebox thursday nights
we forgot seminars
and drank beer and somehow
it turned to she was skinny and smart
so we walked around the block
and ate each other's tongues
to the classroom building
where we had offices
on the third floor we cleared
the desk the married couple shared
and fucked

when the sweat dried
she looked up and said
I like you Charlie
you're a smart guy
and you fill me up
right then I felt it
get hard again inside her
being a sucker for exactly
those two compliments
I slid her to the edge this time
we did it standing up
and the next week
and the next week
clear through to graduation

there should have been a point
but we were young
with too much time
in the stacks
listless with reading
our bodies ached
for what we gave each other
like clockwork
janis on the jukebox
our own simple notion
of what we needed
to survive

True Night

We took the old Chevy out
to the little back road beyond the bluffs
and Craig floored it
    on a long open stretch
under a cloudless
    new moon Colorado sky

We'd been fired from jobs
    we didn't want anyway
and turned down by women
    we didn't love
but still it hurt and we
were feeling nowhere

After a while Craig cut the lights
the way he liked to do
sometimes

and we floated like angels
a touch over a hundred
through the silver-tinged night
toasting our bad fortune
with Pabst Blue Ribbon beer
and singing
old Hank Williams tunes
at the top of our lungs.

Facing East...

After graduate school, the poetry kicked in in a big way. 'Til then I hadn't done much. Now, in Milwaukee where I spent most of the 70s, I met Jeff Winke. Jeff was seriously into haiku, and still is, so I wrote a lot of haiku and still dig it. The first major poetry assignment I gave myself was to sit by the lake every day and write at least one Lake Michigan haiku. The challenge of trying to say something original forced me to work hard at perceiving my environment more closely. The haiku poetic, which forbids interpretation, was good practice for poetry writing in general. After all, it's just another variation of the old "show don't tell," mantra.

Eastern things had always appealed to me. Back in the undergrad days I'd read the UPANISHADS and the BHAGAVAD GITA and also taught myself a little yoga. The Eastern Shore dorm guys couldn't figure it out when I folded my special white sheet, faced the east, and did my daily pranayama (breath) exercises.

In my Milwaukee days, besides the haiku, there was Alan Watts' books on zen, Gary Snyder's translations in RIP RAP AND COLD MOUNTAIN POEMS and Kenneth Rexroth's translations of the Japanese and Chinese poets. Living by the lake also helped. It took me back to childhood, playing in the woods in Morrell Park. I'd lived an urban existence and was missing something. The lake and those Eastern poets brought it back. I haven't loved cities since.

Getting out of my first marriage, the mistake-of-youth marriage, and meeting Mary Ellen, who I'm still with, was another great boost to the quieting that lets the poetry flow. I'm truly indebted to her encouragement then and now and always will be. "loverpoem," the first poem I ever wrote with the flow I was going for, is for and about her.

loverpoem

the basement kitchen
stood up
straight and tall
but you,
you stooped
again and again
getting out the
dinner things
like some great
descending
bird all
grace
and form with
eyes that see
forever
past the simple
solid things you
touch and place
upon
the table or
the roaring flame
with Buddha care
and reverence
you stir the
boiling pots
mix the secret
spices
take the bread and
place it on
the rack, stretch
and breathe and
call to me,
whose poor soul

is spotted
with countless
imperfections
to feast
and be cleansed in
your holy
candlelight

* * * * *

silent moon-filled night;
a thousand sand grains move
to make this footprint

* * * * *

sunrise—
the burial mound's
long shadow

The Kind of Moon it Was
(for Walt)

We arrive early and drink wine
and talk to the waitress
who says she likes Bukowski.
We like that about her
we are feeling monday night.

The ladder is set up
to hold his poems on the shelf
where the paint used to go.

The poet's late
so we look for the waitress

to order more wine, but she's on stage
not looking at all like someone
who likes Bukowski.
She's announcing Walt,
the poet,
is dead.

His friends arrive,
they were in another car.

one
reads from his poems,
another
says a prayer,
the third
chokes on his words

Walt...tonight...Walt...
no...tonight

We forget about poems
and talk about childhood
people we've known, the places.
We order more wine
when the bottle's empty
and after that more wine
and then out
into the cold
Milwaukee night.

I could not tell you what kind of moon it was
or why we each went home alone.

(Walt Cieszynski died on the way to Century Hall to
read his poetry.)

All I Remember About Manitowoc, Wisconsin

is a slim black stripper
with upstanding nipples
and rippling abs
who undulated fiercely
across the dim-lit bar
with a smile
sweet as dusty down south
and home cooking
rare, exotic, transplant
brought north
to dance in dark shadows
in this snow bound town
on the shores of an icy lake
     in northern wisconsin

The February Wisconsin sky

The February Wisconsin sky
was an azure palette
etched with lace and feathers
that burned toward evening
like something out of Blake.
Looking up, it felt as if
my feet grew roots
and that I couldn't move
as if an unseen hand
had moved me
to a better place. Stars appeared

the constellations roared
as I stared, transfixed and tingling
from my little dot in space.

Solitude

The feel on the feet
of pine needle millions
piled up padding the way
through primeval dark
winter late afternoons
when sunlight fades
early and eve turns
quick to night
I like best walking
that time through
pine forest earthdown
alone and unthinking
under heaven's
multiplying stars

A Day In the Life, One of the Better

the plains highlighted in white
        with late spring snow that's been

dusting the front range
        these last three days

ghostly, ice-covered pine
    whiter on windy hilltops

one truck in the last 10 minutes
    —the driver waved

the cut-across road out of Agate
    too rutted by winter winds

we head down undulant SR29
    toward places fringed with magic

Scotts Bluff   the North Platte River
    the Oregon Trail.

(Sioux County, Nebraska, 4/3/99)

Beat Encounters...

In the 80s I was back in the DC area where I met Robert Farr, a young Black poet deeply into the Beats. Robert named our group "Second Wind" because, he said, we were giving the Beat poetic a second wind. To the local established, academic poets, we were street poets, unworthy of attention. We didn't care; we did our own thing. One summer we reserved the stage on the grounds of the Washington Monument, got a sound system, sent out invitations and had an all-day reading attended by friends and random tourists. Other times we'd organize a reading for ourselves or friends in some friendly bar, paste flyers up around town and let it rip. This was in the pre-slam days and regular community venues just didn't exist.

I was past liking cities, but DC put a lot of stuff in my path. I discovered that the Library of Congress sound archives includes poetry as well as music and there, in a sound-proofed room, I heard Kerouac's voice for the first time, heard Gregory Corso read "Bomb" and heard Ferlinghetti read with musical accompaniment. I met Gary Snyder at a literary conference at Frostburg State in western Maryland where he led a meditation session and read from his own work and his recent translations. We sat together for the afternoon Noh play, discussing haiku and other poetic matters as if we'd known each other for years. As a long-time admirer of his work I was delighted that, in person, Gary was as personable and centered as he appears in his writing.

I took a workshop with Allen Ginsberg at a local Shambhala temple which helped loosen up my writing with encouragement toward wild images and hydrogen jukebox juxtapositions. In retrospect, the basic idea of the workshop was simple enough and, of course, profound—"Say Anything," "Let Go," "Let Your Mind Run Wild." It's easy enough to say "First Thought, Best Thought," but it takes a while to become able to do it. That workshop helped move me in the right direction. I think how Allen had been "freed up" by Kerouac's flowing style and feel that he had passed some of that on to me.

There were other inspirational evenings with literary legends. One night Herbert Huncke, a true icon of the Beat era, did a reading at a little natural food cafe in the suburbs. Huncke, the mid-40s hustler-junkie of Times Square, and friend of Kerouac, Burroughs and Ginsberg, was an integral part of the New York scene that helped ignite the Beats. He appears under various names in Clellon Holmes, GO, Kerouac's THE TOWN AND THE CITY and ON THE ROAD, Burrough's JUNKIE, and Ginsberg's HOWL. The evening a small group of fifteen or so of us saw him in Takoma Park he read from his own series of autobiographical story-sketches which are published as THE EVENING SKY TURNED CRIMSON.

Ferlinghetti read at the Writers Center in Bethesda. There was even a celebration of William Burroughs' 70th birthday at a downtown bar with the man himself in attendance. I didn't bother pushing through the honchos and sycophants to talk to him. Just being in the room and seeing this pale, gaunt, spectral self in person was an experience I'll long remember. On another unforgettable night at the Folger Shakespeare Library, James Dickey gave a first-hand demonstration of giving the poetic finger to the establishment. It was supposed to be a workshop and cost ten bucks, no small change in

those days, and here's what happened. After
the pompous introduction by a Library cura-
tor, Dickey lurched to the front of the room
wearing a dirty suede sport coat with one
pocket sagging from the weight of a bottle.
Without introduction, he began a rambling,
semi-coherent talk which lasted a mere 30
minutes during which he punctuated every
few sentences with an emphatic "fuck an' A
right" staring at the front rows of blue-
haired matrons as if daring them to respond.
The room was, shall we say, real quiet. I'd
signed up for the workshop expecting to learn
something about poetry, and I guess I did.
The next day he played it straight at the
reading with nary a "fuck an A" and earned
a standing ovation. As we stood applauding I
wondered if anyone else from the workshop
was in the audience.

On Capitol Hill at the Tune Inn
I Hear America Singing

Sitting Bull has returned,
he's at the drive-in movies
eating up the big screen
demanding hostages,
but everyone ignores him and
goes out for more popcorn.
They're tired of the wobblies and the KKK
they're tired of the black panthers,

they say they're tired of Sitting bull.

Barracuda singles move among
dark booths looking
for fresh meat, Willie Nelson
on the juke box and
across the street congress is debating
intervention.

I hear America singing

Yes, this is America, pardner,
don't you know a free country when you see one?
Come here, son, have yourself a beer
settle down, relax,
this one's on the house
and there's plenty more where that came from,
on the house, plenty more,
    on the house.

Mother Jones turns restless in the earth
Malcolm's old wounds still bleeding
Nam's black wall recalls dead names

Have another beer son,
settle down, this is the voice
of America talking to you,
radio free sixpack.
Don't be so serious, son.
It takes a heap of living to make a planet home.
When we push those little old borders around
it's just sort of like rearranging the furniture,
and them nu-clear bombs, hell boy
ain't nobody fool enough to set one of them
suckers off,

now is there, boy,
I ask you,
now is there?

Everyday Crossroads

At a crossroads in New Mexico
surrounded by open plains
is the little town of Raymond,
where a line of pickup trucks
is parked outside the only bar
night and day.

Not far away, a thin stream
of Rio Grande
runs by,
not at all
the way it looked
in old-time saturday matinees.

Outside the general store
where we bought food to go
and couldn't agree
I look at you and say
don't even think about it.
Even here, the river's,
stronger than it looks.

Then it's your turn to look at me
like a high plains cowboy in a dirty bar
about to pick a fight
he's sure to lose.

Leaving town by a different route
you say the word softly—
"Raymond Raymond"
The word loves your lips
as much as I do.
Then suddenly you turn and say
"that town could have your name."

Downtown in the City of Duck's Blood (Haibun)

Three days on the coast, three days in paterson, nj,
talking poetry to junior high school ghetto kids, walking the streets of closed-down mill town paterson,
meditating on the Great Falls, crossing the river for
a night on the town, oh ghost of william carlos williams oh spirit of ginsberg oh tank-top beauties of
washington square braless in the heat oh congas
and guitars oh city of a million bleeding ducks and
backed up sewers as Lorca called it....

christopher street:
tattoo'd men with three days growth
holding hands

Strolling the East Village after taking the PATH train
into lower Manhattan from Hoboken. Hoboken! My
God, if these people in black only knew, and in fact
they probably do, by the way we look to street signs
for direction, the color of our clothes. Oh fashion, thy
downtown name is

midnight.....

East Village:
mannequins with nipples
in black denim

Amid subway rumble and yellow cab honk the ghost
of Dustin Hoffman's Ratso Rizzo skulks across
Broadway "hey, I'm walking here," the cry of me, the
cry of "I am," straight out of Midnight Cowboy walking
against the light and into the park without a glance
at the woman with orange hair and six rings through
her lower lip, four in each ear and a dozen plastic
necklaces cascading in a rainbow of beads....

corner grocery—
the Asian counterman
greets the customer by name

In the public garden at 6th St. and Avenue B a
woman with gray hair, matted, in ragged skirt and
sweater, bedraggled, pushing a shopping cart among
the flowers, alternately mutters and shouts profani-
ties, cursing the rich, cursing the mayor, cursing the
city, cursing government in general and no one in particular as dog walkers with plastic bags give her wide
berth and two gentlemen in berets discuss perenni-
als and play a slow game of chess inside the gazebo
beside the three-story tall structure of found wood,
baby dolls, and dangling merry-go-round horses....

nightfall:
a sliver of moon
in the skyscraper window

Ceremony at the 42nd St. Library

First go to the information desk
cross the hall to 320
talk to the tall black woman
in the red dress
fill out the application form
complete with personal reference
not a relative
show traceable ID
sign another form and get a card
go down the hall to 316 and
ring the buzzer.
When they let you in
show the card
sign again and state your purpose
take a seat and adjust the light
while the attendant gets your package
sign a final form
hesitate a moment when the box arrives

Then slowly
    s l o w l y
untie the red cotton ribbon
fold back the left flap then right
then top then bottom

there. . .

in the rectangled recess
framed in blue

hesitate again

now

take out five 10-cent pocket notebooks
and read
Kerouac's own penciled hand
OLD ANGEL MIDNIGHT—complete
SCRIPTURES OF THE HOLY ETERNITY—complete
dream fragments play scenes
and other scribbles.
Copy a line you've never seen.
"The moon is a piece of tea"

now
hold the notebooks in your hand
let it all sink in.

Fishing in the Tidal Basin

That morning at the tidal basin
I hooked a fish and Alan caught some haiku
from among the swirling blossoms.
Mermaid scales, he called them
and Matt read from his book of zen poems.

Crows chased after gulls
blossoms stormed the air
and the hundred millionth tourist
took another picture to send home to Omaha.

The fish I caught and released
slid graceful from my hand
sleek and shining
into the dark water

where the ghost of Wilbur Mills
laughts to himself
and the ghost of Fannie Fox
flips a well turned hip
in the direction of the White House
where tricky Dick said "I am not a crook"
and LBJ promised not to escalate
and JFK in an after hours heat
inflated with presidential power
hooked that poor kid, Norma Jean
and never properly let her go.

Scenario

a girl pisses like smoke
through heavy air
on drunken sailors
she's strictly modern

all for the fast breath
the saturday night brawl
sunday morning ache
in the groin
ash in the mouth
bathroom window elegies
the last bar girl
she passes like light
through heavy air
into dawn
knowing and bitten
she's waiting for dark
to return

Performance...

Most of the 1990s I lived in Albany, NY and with Mary Ellen's help (she's got the 9 to 5) I broke from regular employment to the full-time poetry life. In '91, Jack was born and I became an at-home Dad with occasional gigs as a poet in the schools, project director on a grant to bring poetry discussions to libraries in smaller communities around upstate NY, and other freelance poetry gigs. Albany has a great poetry scene, much more than you'd expect for a town of its size. I did more readings there, and in 1993, Dan Wilcox, Tom Nattell, and I formed 3 GUYS FROM ALBANY. Around then, I began making homemade musical instruments and working them into our readings.

By this time the poetry slam scene was going strong. We did feature gigs at a bunch of the major slam venues-places like Cantab Lounge in Cambridge, MA; Nuyorican Poets Cafe in New York, and the Green Mill in Chicago. The beauty of these gigs was that we got to see some of the best slammers around, young poets who present their memorized poems with in-your-face, high-energy delivery. Some of these poets could be grandchildren of the original Beats, but the influence is obvious in their style, attitude and populist approach. Meanwhile we added other performance techniques to our show: multi-voiced poems; audience participation;

wandering around the audience while reciting; and occasional props and costumes.

When I got to Chicago in 1997, poets who know how to write and put across a poem were doing their thing in bars and coffeehouses every night of the week. In '98, Al and I hooked up as AvantRetro. Our show is less eclectic, but more musical than 3 GUYS FROM ALBANY. With Al's musical talents, we use store-bought instruments more often. Besides sax, Al wails a mean flute. I bring my conga drum along with the cake cover gong, candlestick chimes and mojo rhythm stick that I use with 3 GUYS. But despite the accompanying whatever, we always keep the focus on the poem. The performance techniques are only there to help the poem get across. One thing we've noticed regardless of the audience, a lot of the poems that work best in performance are those with a strong Beat influence; they're accessible, rhythmic, personal, honest and they seek that elusive spiritual something that's lurking out there somewhere beneath the surface of this tangible world we live in.

Who We Are

the neighbor's retarded boys sits
in the back seat of the family car
ever so gently love me now rocking,
a cold wind off the lake (love me now)
rustles the love me now leaves,
a dog's bark echoes through
an empty house of love me now (love me now)
the grocery store clerk smiles
her have a nice day love me now smile,

           (love me now)
the cop on the corner waves the kids
across the love me now avenue,
and behind closed doors up and down
this trim lawn tree-lined street a hundred
intimate love me now gestures over

(love me now)
love me now kitchen tables
and love me now tricycles
in love me now family rooms sing (love me now)
in thousand-part harmony
the singular unbending
      (love me now)
universal love me now
anthem of who we are

("Who We Are" PERFORMANCE NOTE: (parentheses) indicates 2nd voice. 1st voice does not wait for 2nd voice. Occasionally both voices speak simultaneously. Spaces between lines are to clarify performance; there are no stanza breaks.)

Divorce

we were
three weeks
together
somewhere
her husband
waved
a gun
when she
told him
but didn't fire
into the phone
I moved
out, out,
my first wife
was no good
for me and
emotions
make me
nervous
I barely
recall
the rest
that wife
my hair
in the shower
but the one
with the husband
with the gun
who one day
stopped
returning my calls
she is indelible
as birth

and Erika
my daughter
she was one
at the time
she was one
she was
one.

The Ex

She's the worst kind of monster
made up of old parts of yourself
that needed a woman like her
and couldn't see disaster looming

like a bad dream that keeps coming back
when you let your guard down
you see her in a dark cafe and shiver,
it's like a visit from the grave
you try to recall good times
but you're torn—how else
to justify
how else to move on

you've switched back to your old brand
of toothpaste, but you still wear
clothes you wore with her
and drive the same car. You wonder

how far you'll have to go.
You want to blame it all on her
then you want to blame it all on you.
In your better moments you wish her well.

The First Week

Breakfast got away,
lunch was thin grilled cheese
on the run, and dinner was late

      He eats like clockwork and sleeps
      like Bucky Fuller, 2 or 3 hours
      at a stretch

We count diapers to be sure
he's ok, boil water
to sterilize things

      He looks around a little
      cries to be fed, eats again and
        dozes off
After our first stroll in the woods
      I tried him on some old songs.
            Howling Wolf, Hank Williams,
            Woody Guthrie.
    They blew through the trees like a choir
of angels. Then I put my feet up
           opened a beer and we both fell
           asleep
                in the big cedar chair.

In Cars. . .

I've slept, dreamed, yelled, cried, laughed, lied,
loitered and sighed

I've been lost, wasted, hugged, hated, kissed, missed,
puzzled, pissed, loved, laughed at and
    berated

I've been scared, impaired, rich, bored, sad, poor, ex-
plored, tired, wired, desired, hungry, horny,
        denied, and satisfied

I've sung four part harmony waiting for the light and
blown blues harp in the key of C

I've played poker, blackjack, chess, gin rummy and old
license plate games of time

I've gnashed teeth and kicked dashboard in start
goddamn it cold morning frustration

I've talked ambitious truth, abandoned all logic and
lived in the heart

I've driven long macho road trips 30 hours straight
with all night diner coffee and head out
    the window crack of dawn

I've had wonderful sex in front seat and back from interstate blow job to ski pants rutting
        fuck in the parka afternoon

I've spent long nights at the drive-in where I ripped
out my share of speakers with forgetful

sputter and squawk

I've been here to there and back again
In cars that are new, swift, strong
In cars that are old, ragged, worn,
In cars with doors that won't open, bald tires,
        fender dents and rust,
In cars with doors that won't close, bad wires,
        broken heaters and locks
In cars with warm headlights
In cars with cloud cushions
In cars with dream dashboards
In cars that freeze childhood
In cars that kiss danger
In cars that feed angels
In cars.....in cars.....in cars.

I Dropped the Bomb

I
  I
   I
I dropped
I dropped
I dropped the bomb
I dropped the bomb
I dropped the bomb because
I dropped the bomb because I was confused
    I was looking for a light
     and the button was right there shining.
I dropped the bomb because I was curious
    I was looking for a fix of the new.

Haven't you ever put your finger
where it doesn't belong
just to have an experience?
I dropped the bomb because it's faster than booze.
Who wants an alchy slow rot death
when you can go out in a blaze
like something that really matters.
I dropped the bomb because space is the final frontier
and it's time to move on.
Nobody loves a dead planet;
it's time for a shot at the stars.
I dropped the bomb because I was a nice boy
who needed to express himself.
I craved the stardom of the 5 o'clock news.
I forgot it wouldn't be there.
I was tired of being good;
I knew there was more to me than that.
I dropped the bomb because it rhymes with tomb
and we're all unknown soldiers.
We all fight for something.
What did you stand up for today?
I dropped the bomb because somebody asked me to
and I'm the ingratiating type.
I thought it was a way to make friends,
but there's no justice
and who wants to live
in an unjust world.
I dropped the bomb because bombs were made
to be dropped,
guns are made to be shot,
doors are made to be opened.
I dropped the bomb because I was horny
and needed to get laid.
I'd been without it for days,
I was ready to explode

and relief was nowhere in sight.
I dropped the bomb because I wanted to save the
 world.
  It's a dirty job
  but somebody's got to do it
  and besides, it's an outlet for my
   Messiah complex.
I dropped the bomb because Adam and Eve ate
 that apple
  Christianity made me do it.
  All that incense I sniffed must have gone
   to my head.
  I was in a spiritual haze.
  I thought I saw God
  He was up in the clouds saying
  Do it! Do it! Do it!
  and a whole chorus of angels was saying
  Do it! Do it! Do it!
  and the Virgin Mary in a string bikini was saying
  Do it! Do it! Do it!
  and I wanted to do it
  Oh God how I wanted to do it.
I dropped the bomb because somebody said shit
 or get off the pot
  and I'm a man of action.
I dropped the bomb because I'm an American.
I dropped the bomb to impress the girls.
I dropped the bomb to show them I'm no wimp.
I dropped the bomb to show them I'm a real man.

A Final Nod to Roots...

Han Shan was, as Gary Snyder put it, "a mountain madman in an old Chinese line of ragged hermits" who lived roughly 1,300 years ago on Cold Mountain, from which he took his name. Lu Ch'iu-Yin, in a preface to a collection of Han Shan's poems, said the poet looked like an old ragged tramp yet "every word he breathed was a meaning in line with the subtle principles of things, if only you thought of it deeply. Every word he said had a feeling of the Tao in it."

Inspired by Han Shan's attitude and poetry I wrote my own sequence of Cold Mountain poems, placing the poet in a contemporary urban setting. These poems are my tribute to a man who embodies some of the most important and appealing aspects of the Beat ethos—fierce individuality and independence, combined with sincere spiritual questing, expressed in a poetry of everyday language. Han Shan was a man who, beneath a self-effacing and often seemingly frivolous exterior, was an earnest seeker of the Way. The complete "Cold Mountain 2000" series consists of twenty four poems which directly parallel the twenty-four Cold Mountain poems by Han Shan as translated by Gary Snyder and presented in Snyder's book RIPRAP AND COLD MOUNTAIN POEMS. In performance, I typically do a handful of poems from the series with accompaniment by Al on bamboo flute.

Cold Mountain 2,000:
Han Shan in the City (selections)

1

The way to this place is laughable,
there's no straight path.
Grubby streets and back alleys
littered and grungy.
Citizens pass on the way to work
from my old neighborhood
but I've lost the shortcut home.
Sometimes I just sit and wonder
where it all leads.

3

It's bleak here
it's always been bleak.
Dark buildings half-blown down,
shadows enough to spook a saint.
But grass still sprouts each June
school kids return each autumn.
Now I'm here, which is nowhere
looking for a vision that's hard to come by

6

People ask how to get here
but it's tricky business—
the way keeps changing.
When you're depressed
you think it's close by
when you're elated
you think you might already be here.

If your heart was like mine
you wouldn't need a mood to find the way.

14

This neighborhood has many wonders
but people who come here get scared.
When the street lights shine
and the gangs are out
things don't look the way
they look in daylight.
But when it rains, the reflections
on the street are like rainbows
I swear it
they're like rainbows.

The Great Fixations
(Love, Longing, Death)

it's all about isn't it
me and hold me
anyone will do

longing is the basic state
we shiver through
inevitable as weather

winds blow, trees fall
and we try to stay standing
but that's all vanity

nature happens,
averages, I don't want them
for me, not that way

I don't want to go
typically with yet
so many things to do

undone

Patrons of CR+P #15 & Broadside #1

Tom & Judy Amberg

Anonymous (E.R.P)

Anonymous (G.E.B)

Anonymous (N.F.R.)

Anonymous (S.O.L.)

Sharon Auberle

Roy Bergold

Gary Busha/WOLFSONG PRESS, Sturtevant WI

Charles F. Calkins/THE BADGER BIBLIOPHILE, Books & Maps,
    Waukesha WI

Robin Chapman

Patt Clark

Barbara Collins

Alice D'Alessio

Stephen Dunker/WHAT GOES 'ROUND, Books, Bayfield WI

Robert Farr

Richard Finch

Sandra Friedman

Jude Genereaux

Chris Halla/SHAGBARK PRESS, Appleton WI

Tina Harper

Richard Hougen

Emmett Johns

Lars Johnson

Lowell B. Komie/SWORD-FISH-CHICAGO PRESS

DyAnne Korda/Scott Stowell

Bobbie Krinsky

Jackie Langetieg

Donna Lash/THE BRIDGE, Books, Egg Harbor WI

Tom Montag

Gladyce Nahbenayash

Edith Nash

Peg Nemeth

Tom Nicotera

Carol Ordal

Maggie Perry

Elizabeth Pochron/SIGNS OF LIFE, Astrologer

Ralph Rausch

Mariann Ritzer

Marty & Mary Robinson

Paul Schroeder

Pedro & Kathi Villarreal

Cindy Voorhies

Barbara Vroman

Sharry & Bob Wershay

Dan Wilcox